Franklin Has a Sleepover

Kids Can Press Ltd. acknowledges with appreciation the
assistance of the Canada Council and the Ontario Arts
Council in the production of this book.

Canadian Cataloguing in Publication Data

Bourgeois, Paulette
    Franklin has a sleepover

ISBN 1-55074-300-7 (bound) ISBN 1-55074-302-3 (pbk.)

1. Picture books for children.   I. Clark, Brenda.   II. Title.

PS8553.085477F73 1996   jC813'.54   C95-932103-9
PZ7.B68Fr 1996

Kids Can Press Ltd.
29 Birch Avenue
Toronto, Ontario, Canada
M4V 1E2

Printed and bound in Hong Kong
by Wing King Tong Company Limited

96 0 9 8 7 6 5 4 3 2 1

Franklin Has a Sleepover

Paulette Bourgeois
Brenda Clark

Kids Can Press Ltd., Toronto

FRANKLIN could count by twos and tie his shoes. He could zip zippers and button buttons. He could even sleep alone in his small, dark shell. So Franklin thought he was ready for his first sleepover. He asked his mother if Bear could stay overnight.

"All right," said Franklin's mother. "But where will Bear sleep?"

Franklin's room was small for a turtle *and* a bear.

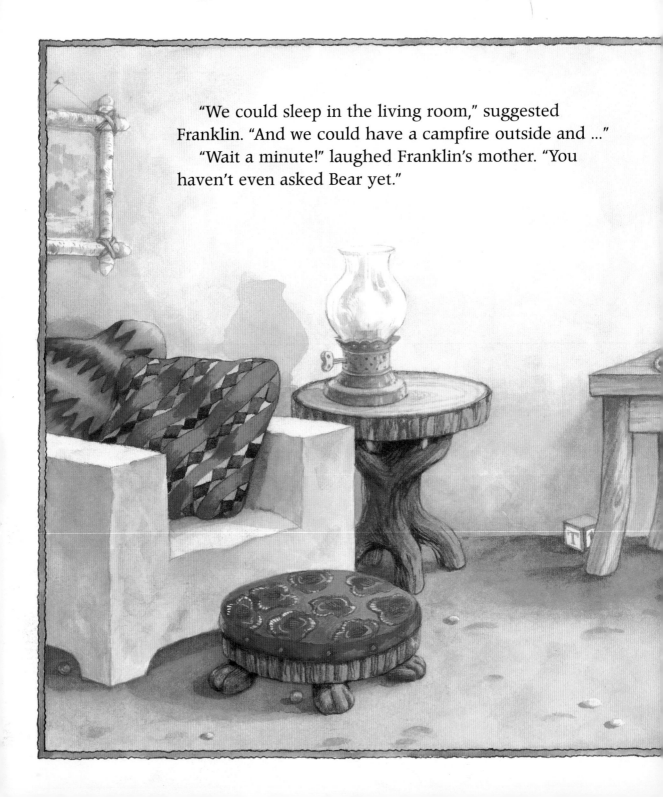

"We could sleep in the living room," suggested Franklin. "And we could have a campfire outside and ..."

"Wait a minute!" laughed Franklin's mother. "You haven't even asked Bear yet."

Bear did a happy dance after Franklin called.
"May I please go?" he asked.

His parents worried that the two friends would keep each other awake all night.

"We'll sleep," promised Bear.

Then they wondered if he would feel homesick.

"Not me!" said Bear.

So his parents said yes.

Bear called Franklin. "I can come! I can come!" he shouted.

Franklin could hardly wait. Bear wouldn't arrive until after supper, and Franklin had just finished lunch. So he sorted all his toys and picked Bear's favourites. He made sure there was enough to eat. He even tidied his room. Franklin wanted everything to be just right for his first sleepover.

Bear was excited, too. He couldn't decide what to bring and what to leave behind. He filled an enormous bag with toys, books, a pillow, a sleeping bag, a puzzle and a flashlight. He packed slippers, a toothbrush and a snack. He put his bunny on top of the bag. And every hour he asked if it was time to go.

After supper, Franklin sat by the window, waiting for his friend. Finally, Bear and his parents arrived.

"Have a good time," they said. Bear gave them each a great big hug.

"We're camping in the living room," said Franklin.

"Oh, I've never done that before," said Bear.

He laid out his sleeping bag and Franklin made a tent from a tablecloth.

"This is going to be so much fun," giggled Bear.

They played all their favourite games. Before long it was dark outside.

"How about a campfire?" asked Franklin's father.

"With marshmallows?" Bear licked his lips.

"And hot dogs too," said Franklin's mother.

Franklin's father told Bear and Franklin what to do. They gathered sticks and twigs at the edge of the woods and helped to lay the fire. They filled a bucket with sand and another with water.

"I'll light the fire," said Franklin's mother.

There was a crackle, and sparks jumped into the air.

"I went to camp," said Franklin's father. "We used to sing while the fire was burning."

He sang in a clear, low voice. By the end of the song, Franklin and Bear had learned all the words. The frogs in the pond were croaking, and the owl in the woods was hooting.

Franklin and Bear toasted marshmallows and roasted hot dogs. Bear had two of everything. Then for a long, long time they sat quietly, watching the stars.

Franklin yawned and Bear rubbed his eyes.

"Time to put out the fire and go inside," said Franklin's father.

When Franklin and Bear were ready for bed,
Franklin's parents gave them both a glass of water
and a good-night hug.

"Sleep tight," they said, turning off the light.

The two friends lay still for a moment. Then
Bear turned on his flashlight.

"Franklin?" he whispered. "I don't feel good."

"Did you eat too much?" asked Franklin.

"No," sniffed Bear. A tear ran down his cheek.

"What's wrong then?"

Bear looked around. "I miss my room."

"Oh," said Franklin. Then he had an idea. "Bring your bed and come with me. We can sleep in my room."

Bear found a cosy spot and snuggled into his sleeping bag. After a moment, he turned on his flashlight again.

"What's wrong now?" Franklin asked.

"My mother always says good night to my bunny," whispered Bear.

So Franklin gave the bunny a hug. "Good night, Bunny. Good night, Bear," he said.

Soon they were fast asleep.

The next morning, Franklin's father made them a special breakfast.

"Did you have a nice sleepover?" asked Franklin's mother.

"It was wonderful," said Bear. "Thank you. Next time, may Franklin come to my house?"

"Of course," Franklin's parents laughed.
Franklin did his own happy dance.
"And, Bear," said Franklin, tapping his shell,
"don't worry about where I will sleep. I always
bring my own cosy bed with me!"